Enid Blyton

The Cat with a Feathery Tail

...and other stories

Bounty
Books

Published in 2015 by Bounty Books,
a division of Octopus Publishing Group Ltd,
Carmelite House
50 Victoria Embankment,
London EC4Y 0DZ
www.octopusbooks.co.uk

An Hachette UK Company
www.hachette.co.uk
Enid Blyton ® Text copyright © 2011 Chorion Rights Ltd.
Illustrations copyright © 2015 Award Publications Ltd.
Layout copyright © 2015 Octopus Publishing Group Ltd.

Illustrated by Lesley Smith.

ISBN: 978-0-75372-954-0

A CIP catalogue record for this book is available from the
British Library.

Printed and bound in the United Kingdom

3 5 7 9 10 8 6 4

CONTENTS

The Cat
with a Feathery Tail

There was once a cat who longed to catch the birds that flew about the garden. But the birds knew Tinker very well, and whenever he appeared, they always flew away.

It didn't matter where Tinker hid, the birds always found out. It was the blackbird who always seemed to see him hiding under the bushes.

"Beware, beware, beware!" the blackbird would cry in his loud voice. "Cat in the bushes! Cat in the bushes!"

Then all the birds would fly off at once, and Tinker would sit up and glare at the blackbird sitting at the top of the hazel tree.

Tinker's paws were velvety and soft. He made no noise when he ran. But however softly he went, the birds

always knew he was coming.

"Cat!" they cried to one another. "Chirrup, chirrup! Here's the cat!"

The other cats laughed at Tinker. "Birds are not so easy to catch as you think!" they said. "Leave them alone. They do you no harm. You have plenty of dinner to eat without worrying the birds."

But Tinker longed and longed to catch

the birds. He sat and thought for a long time how he might manage to get one.

Now the little boy he belonged to had a Red Indian hat. He sometimes wore it in the garden, and he looked very grand indeed when he did. It was made of green and yellow feathers, and was really magnificent.

Tinker saw this hat in the toy-cupboard one day when he was in the nursery, and an idea came into his clever mind.

"Suppose I get some of those feathers and tie them to my long tail," he thought. "Then I could lie down in the garden, curl my feathery tail over my body to hide me – and I would look like some kind of bird!"

The more he thought about this, the more he felt it was a splendid idea. So he bit out eight of the bright feathers and ran off with them to the garden shed. He got some of the string that the gardener kept there, and very cleverly managed to tie those feathers all along his tail. My, they did look funny, I can tell you!

Then out into the sunshine went Tinker, his long feathery tail dragging behind him. The cat went to the middle of the lawn and

lay down. He curled his curious tail over his body, so that the feathers stood up and made him look like a peculiar kind of bird.

He kept quite still. Soon the blackbird saw him and cocked his head on one side as he balanced himself on the fence.

"Look at that, look at that!" called the blackbird. "What is it? A peacock? No! A kingfisher? No! Then what is it?"

The other birds flew down to look. They simply could not imagine what this curious bundle of feathers was. They felt sure it must be a new kind of bird.

They hopped a little closer. The sparrows put their brown heads on one side and watched carefully. The peculiar bird didn't move. It was very strange.

"Let's go right up to it and ask it what sort of bird it is," said the chaffinch. "I've never seen one quite like it before."

The cat was pleased. Aha, it would soon be able to jump up and catch five or six birds at once!

And then Fluffy, the next-door cat, jumped up on to the wall and caught sight of the peculiar bundle of feathers too. He was really astonished!

"Now what bird is that?" he thought. "I must go and see."

So he jumped down to the lawn and strolled over the grass. At once all the sparrows, the two chaffinches, the blackbird, and the thrush flew off in a fright.

"Beware, beware!" sang out the blackbird in his ringing voice. "Cat on the grass! Cat on the grass!"

Tinker peered through his feathers and saw Fluffy. What a nuisance! Fluffy had frightened away the birds. Perhaps if he lay quite still, Fluffy would go away, and then the birds would come back again.

So he lay as still as could be and only his feathery tail waved a little in the wind. Fluffy sat down to look at it.

He simply couldn't make out what kind of bird it was. He called to Paddy-Paws, the cat who lived in the house at the bottom of the garden.

"Paddy-Paws! Fetch Tibs and Tabby and come and look at this strange creature."

Paddy-Paws went off and fetched Tibs and Tabby. They were two grey tabbies. All four cats sat down and watched the bright feathery tail blowing in the wind. "Did you ever see a bird like this before?" said Fluffy.

"It doesn't seem to have a head," said Tibs.

"It seems to be mostly tail," said Tabby.

"It's not a bit afraid of us," said Paddy.

"It doesn't fly away."

"I expect it would if we got a bit closer," said Fluffy. "Birds always do."

"Well, what about pouncing on it and catching it," whispered Tibs. "It doesn't seem to be moving. I think it is asleep. Let's try to catch it!"

"Right!" said Paddy. "Now – one – two – three – GO!"

All four cats leapt at the same time on to

poor Tinker. He wasn't expecting that at all. He got a dreadful shock when he felt the four cats jump on to him. They dug their claws into him and Tibs bit him hard on the ear.

"Get away! You horrid things!" mewed Tinker, struggling hard and putting out all his twenty claws at once.

The cats were so excited that at first they didn't hear Tinker mewing. They scratched him hard. Feathers flew off his tail and danced about the lawn.

"Stop, stop!" cried Tinker, biting and

scratching. "I'm a cat, not a bird! Leave me alone!"

The four cats leapt off Tinker in surprise. "Good gracious! It's Tinker!" said Fluffy.

"What have you dressed yourself up in feathers for?" said Tibs.

"Is this a new game or something?" said Tabby, disgusted. "What are you lying about the grass dressed up in yellow and green feathers for?"

"To catch the birds," said poor Tinker, licking his scratches. "You spoilt everything. I think you are silly, stupid, unkind things. You gave me a terrible

13

shock when you jumped on me like that and dug your claws into me. Go away. I don't like you."

The four cats went away, laughing. The blackbird sat on top of the fence and called to Tinker.

"Now you know what a bird feels like when a cat springs on it and digs her claws in! Serves you right, Tinker, serves you right!"

Tinker felt foolish. He washed himself and pretended to take no notice. But

suddenly the little boy to whom Tinker belonged ran out into the garden. He had seen the torn feathers, and was very angry.

"You took them out of my Red Indian hat!" he cried. "You're a bad, bad cat! I shall smack you!"

And he did smack Tinker – slap, slap, slap! The surprised cat gave loud meows and ran away to hide. The blackbird sat on the top of the fence and called the news to all the other birds.

"The cat's getting smacked! Hurrah! The cat's getting smacked! Come and see-ee-ee! Come and see-ee-ee!"

And they all came to see-ee-ee. Poor Tinker! He never once tried to catch a bird after that!

A Bit of
Good Luck

"Mary! Have you seen my little gold watch anywhere?" called Granny.

Mary ran indoors to Granny. "No, I haven't," she said. "Oh dear. Have you lost it, Granny?"

"It must have slipped off my wrist when I was weeding in the garden," said Granny. "Could you look for it, dear?"

"Yes, of course," said Mary, and ran out again to hunt for the watch. She looked in all the beds that Granny had weeded. She looked in the tool shed where Granny had gone to fetch flower-pots. She looked in the lettuce bed, because she knew Granny had picked a fat, crisp lettuce for tea.

But the little gold watch was nowhere to be found. What a pity!

"I did love it so much," said Granny sadly. "Grandpa gave it to me forty years ago – think of that! It has never once stopped going all those years. Now it will lie out in the cold and rain, and will very soon stop ticking out the time."

"Oh, Granny, what bad luck!" said Mary. "You haven't had good luck lately, you know. You broke the red bowl you love so much – and you tore your new dress and spoilt it. I wish I could bring you some good luck!"

"Nobody can do that," said Granny. "Well, thank you, dear, for hunting about for my watch. Off you go into the sunshine again. I'll call you when it's dinnertime."

Mary went out. She was staying a

17

whole week with Granny, and she liked it. Granny was kind and good, and she loved a little joke. Mary *wished* that she could find the treasured little gold watch.

"I wish I could find some good luck for Granny, too," she thought. "Oh – I *wonder* if I could find a four-leaved clover? Four-leaved clovers are very, very lucky; there must be magic in them, I suppose. Yes, I think I'll look for one."

But it wasn't very easy, because Granny's little lawn was so well kept that there were no patches of clover leaves there at all – and hardly even a daisy, but just soft green grass.

"Well, perhaps there will be some clover leaves in the orchard," thought Mary, and she went to where apple and pear trees stood in the grassy little orchard. She was soon hunting for clover.

"Oh, there's lots here!" she said, in delight, and she began to look through the big clover patches.

She hunted and hunted. Every leaf she found was cut into three! Mary began to get tired of looking carefully at every patch.

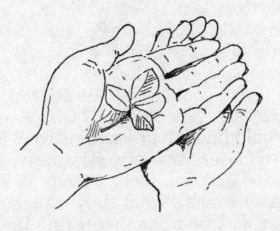

Then she suddenly found a four-leaved clover – you can see it in the picture! It's a beauty, isn't it? Mary was very happy.

"Oh! Here's one at last – in this big, thick patch of leaves. I must have looked at hundreds – and now I've found a four-leaved one!"

Then she found something else! She saw something shining in the very middle of the thick clump of clover. And would you believe it – it was Granny's little gold watch!

"Well! That just *shows* that four-leaved

clovers are lucky!" said Mary happily. "No sooner do I find one than I find the lost watch, too! How pleased Granny will be!"

She ran to the house, holding the watch in one hand and the four-leaved clover in the other. "Granny! Look what I've got!"

Granny came to the door. "Oh, Mary! You've found my watch. Where was it?" she cried.

"In the orchard – in the middle of a patch of clover," said Mary. "And it's still ticking away, Granny. You just put it to your ear and listen. It didn't mind being dropped. Wasn't it lucky that I found it?"

"It was," said Granny, putting the watch on her wrist.

"And do you know why I found it?" said Mary. "I found a four-leaved clover just a minute before – and that's a very lucky thing to find isn't it? It brought me luck at once, because then I found the watch, you see!"

She held out the four-leaved clover to Granny. "You can have it, Granny darling. You want some good luck, I know, and I'm glad I've got some to give you. You can have the four-leaved clover for yourself."

"You're a pet," said Granny, and she took the little four-leaved clover. "I shall put it my diary and look at it every day. But are you sure you don't want to keep it yourself? Wouldn't you like some good luck?"

"I want *you* to have it," said Mary. "I found it for you, really, you know."

Granny kissed her. "Well," she said, "whatever good luck comes along while you are staying with me you shall share!"

And believe it or not, that very same day a friend brought Granny an enormous box of chocolates, so Mary had half of them!

The day after that Daddy came to see Granny and Mary, and brought a big slab of ice-cream for Granny. So Mary had to have half of that.

And the third day somebody sent Granny tickets for a Grand Show at the Town Hall – with a Punch and Judy show, puppets and a conjurer!

"One ticket for me – and one for you!" said Granny, giving one to Mary. "Your four-leaved clover is certainly bringing me luck, Mary!"

"And me, too!" said Mary joyfully. "I gave my four-leaved clover luck to you, Granny – and *I'm* getting lots of luck too!"

"You deserve it, Mary!" said Granny. And so she did!

The Girl
Who Had Hiccups

There was once a little girl who often got hiccups when she laughed. I expect you get them sometimes, don't you? They are funny things to have.

Well, Sheila often had them, and she called them hee-cups. I don't know if you call them hee-cups, too. Quite a lot of people do.

Anyway, Sheila was always saying, "Oh! I've got the hee-cups again! Mummy, can I have a lump of sugar to suck?"

That was such a nice cure for the hee-cups. A lump of sugar is delicious to have in your mouth. First it is hard and knobbly. Then it goes soft and sweet. Then it melts altogether and, as Sheila said, you end by drinking it down your throat.

"You *are* lucky to have so many hee-cups, Sheila," her friends said to her. "You are always having lumps of sugar to suck!"

Now one day, when Sheila was walking home over Cuckoo Hill, she saw the wind take off the scarecrow's hat nearby, and that made her laugh. She laughed and she laughed.

And then she got hiccups! You know the sort of funny noise you keep making, don't you, when you've got hiccups? You just can't help it. Something seems to catch your breath and you make a noise in your throat.

"I've got the hee-cups!" cried Sheila, as

she skipped along over the hill. "I've got the hee-cups! Oh!"

Then something surprising happened. A small man ran out from behind a tree and went up to Sheila. He had on a blue tunic, and he had pointed ears and slanting green eyes.

"I say! Have you really got some cups?" he asked. "Where are they? We've just broken ours, and we did so want a picnic."

Sheila looked down in surprise. "Are you a brownie, or something?" she asked.

"Yes, of course," said the little fellow.

"But what about those cups you were shouting about just now?"

"Oh, they were hee-cups I was saying I had got," said Sheila, with a giggle.

"Well, wouldn't those do to drink from?" said the brownie, pulling at Sheila's hand. "My friends and I would be so pleased if you would lend them to us. Just for half an hour. Please do. If you will, you can share our picnic."

Well, Sheila thought it would be marvellous to share in a brownie's picnic. She looked around and saw five more little men peeping out from behind the trees. Some were dressed in blue and some in brown. They all had pointed ears and slanting eyes.

"Listen," said Sheila. "I would lend you my hee-cups if I could – but I can't."

"Oh, don't be mean," said the brownie. "How many have you got?"

"Oh, hundreds I should think!" said Sheila.

"Have they got handles?" asked the brownie.

"Mine haven't," said Sheila, beginning to giggle again.

"How funny!" said the brownie, puzzled. "Is there a pretty pattern on them?"

"I shouldn't think so," said Sheila, and she giggled again. Then she gave a very loud hee-cup. She looked at the little man.

"That was a hee-cup!" she said. "Didn't you see it? Or did you only hear it?"

"I didn't see anything," said the brownie. "I think you are rather an unkind little girl to say you've got such a lot of cups – and yet you won't lend us any. You see, Jinky fell down and broke all ours – and we have some most delicious honey-lemonade to drink."

"I've never tasted that," said Sheila, feeling that she would very much like to. Then a great idea came into her mind. She couldn't give the brownie her hee-cups to put lemonade in, but if they would wait a few minutes she could fetch cups from her dolls' teaset!

"You just wait a minute and I'll fetch you some cups," she said. And off she sped, running home as fast as ever she could.

She took seven cups. They were white with pink roses round. Back she went to Cuckoo Hill. The six brownies were waiting for her, smiles all over their faces. They had spread a little cloth on the grass and had set out exciting-looking sandwiches and buns. There was a tall jug of honey-lemonade too.

"Oh! She's brought her hee-cups for us after all!" cried the blue brownie, delighted. "Aren't they pretty?"

Sheila set out the cups. They did look sweet. The brownies really loved them. They poured Sheila a cup of their honey-lemonade at once. She tasted it – and it was simply delicious.

"We do like your little hee-cups," said the brownies, pleased. "They are lovely hee-cups. Have a sandwich?"

Sheila had seven sandwiches and five buns and four cups of honey-lemonade. Then the brownie washed the seven cups in the nearby stream, and gave them back to Sheila.

"Thank you very much," they said. "You *are* lucky to have such nice hee-cups!"

Sheila laughed – and her hee-cups came back again. She kept making the kind of noise you have to make when you have hiccups.

"Are you ill or just being rude?" the brownies asked her solemnly. That made Sheila laugh all the more – and her hiccups got much worse. She shouted good-bye and ran home with her little dolls' cups.

"Mummy, I've got hee-cups, please may I have a lump of sugar?" she said. She got her lump of sugar and sucked it, to make the hiccups go.

She put her dolls' cups back into the tea-set box. "I expect the brownies will always call you hee-cups!" she said.

And they do! You should hear them talking about them.

"We had lemonade in Sheila's hee-cups," they tell their friends. "Oh, you should have seen her dear little hee-cups! We're going to buy some for ourselves if we can!"

But they won't be able to, will they?

I'll Do Them Tomorrow

Linnie was a plump little pixie girl who lived in a tiny cottage in the middle of Pat-a-cake Village. It was a pretty little cottage, with red and pink roses climbing outside, and big hollyhocks waving by the walls.

But inside the cottage was very different! Goodness me, how dirty it was! The floor wanted scrubbing. The curtains wanted washing. The windows wanted cleaning, and everything looked as if it needed a good brushing and dusting.

"You *are* a lazy little thing, Linnie," said her neighbour, Dame Trot-About. "Why don't you clean your kettle and your saucepans?"

"Linnie, why don't you do a little hard work?" cried her other neighbour, Mother Lucy. "Look at your curtains!

They are a disgrace to the village!"

"I'll do them tomorrow," promised Linnie. But she didn't. She never did any work if she could help it, the lazy little thing.

Then one day her Aunt Jemima sent her twenty-five pence to spend, and Linnie made up her mind to ask old Mrs Redhands to come along and clean her house for her.

"She will do it for twenty-five pence," thought Linnie. "And then my neighbours will perhaps stop worrying me about my dirty cottage. I'll call in and ask her today."

Mrs Redhands said yes, certainly she would come along and clean Linnie's cottage for twenty-five pence. So she arrived the next day in a big clean apron and knocked at the door. Linnie opened it. "Come along in!" she said. "I'm afraid the cottage is rather dirty – but, you see, I haven't had time to clean it for some weeks."

Mrs Redhands looked round the rooms. "Good gracious!" she said in disgust. "I never saw such a mess in my life. I can't do all this in a day. You will have to let me come tomorrow as well."

"But I can't pay you for two days," said Linnie.

"Well, you must help me, then," said Mrs Redhands. "First of all, where's the soap and the scrubbing brush?"

"I forgot to get the soap," said Linnie, "but here's the scrubbing-brush." She held out a very old one and Mrs Redhands shook her head at once.

"No use at all," she said. "You must go out and get a new one – and some soap, too. Now hurry, for goodness sake, because I want to start!"

She rushed Linnie out of the front door, and the pixie ran quite fast. She bought the soap, a scrubbing-brush, a new broom, and a duster, for she was afraid that Mrs Redhands would think she needed those too.

"Now go and fill the pail with hot water for me!" cried Mrs Redhands, rolling her sleeves up. "Hurry, Linnie! Bring it to me here – and put some more coal on the fire, please, to keep the water hot."

Linnie filled the pail and carried it to Mrs Redhands, puffing and panting. Then she put some coal on the fire. After that she picked up the paper and sat down to read it.

"Linnie, Linnie!" called Mrs Redhands. "Come and clear this room for me. I can't scrub the floor with all these rugs about.

Roll them up for me and take them into the garden. And you might hang them on the line and give them a bang to get the dust out."

Linnie went to roll up the rugs. They were so dusty that they made her cough. She hung them on the line and then fetched the carpet-beater. But she didn't like the hard work and soon gave it up.

"Can't you beat the carpets properly?" called Mrs Redhands. "Well, I'll do that for you – but you must clean away the cobwebs from the ceiling if I do that. Here's the broom."

Linnie found herself sweeping away heaps of cobwebs. They fell on her pretty golden hair. She was horrified to see how many cobwebs there were. She wrapped

a hanky round her head, and swept away some more cobwebs.

"Oh dear! Why ever did I let my cottage get so dirty?" she thought. "Oooh – there's a great big spider. Go away, Eight-Legs, go away!"

The spider ran straight at Linnie, and she called to Mrs Redhands. "Oh, come and finish doing the cobwebs – I don't like spiders."

"Well, I've finished the rugs, so I'll come and do the ceilings," said Mrs Redhands, bustling in. "Now, my dear, what's for dinner? I do a good morning's work and it makes me hungry. I'm not having anything out of a tin, let me tell you – I want a well-cooked dinner."

"Well, what would you like to cook?" asked Linnie.

"My dear, *you're* going to do the cooking!" said Mrs Redhands. "Don't make any mistake about that! I've come here to clean your dirty cottage, not to cook a dinner for myself."

So Linnie had to peel potatoes, fetch some chops from the butcher, and get ready a steamed treacle pudding. Goodness, she hadn't worked so hard for months!

She did enjoy her dinner – just as much as Mrs Redhands did. Afterwards she

had to wash up, and then Mrs Redhands called her.

"Linnie! These curtains must be washed. They are so black that I don't know what colour they are supposed to be! Take them all down and put them in to soak for me whilst I finish cleaning out this room."

"Oh dear!" thought Linnie, running to get the washtub. "How hard I am working today! Why ever did I get Mrs Redhands in? I'm doing more work today than I did for weeks."

She took down all the curtains. She put them to soak. Then she found that she had let the kitchen fire out; and as Mrs

Redhands said she really must have more hot water, Linnie had to light it again. Then she had to give Mrs Redhands a hand in hanging out the curtains.

"They will be dry enough to iron after tea," said Mrs Redhands happily. "You and I can do that together, Linnie."

"Oh dear! Can't they be left till tomorrow?" said Linnie. "I'm so tired."

"Tired! Nonsense! You've had quite a lazy day compared with me," said Mrs Redhands. "And I shouldn't *think* of leaving the curtains. Very lazy thing to do. That's what's been the matter with you, Linnie, I can see – you leave things till tomorrow – and then they never get done. No wonder your cottage is the dirtiest in the whole of the village."

Linnie went red. She didn't like hearing that. She put the irons on the stove to warm and hoped that the curtains wouldn't take long to do.

But good Mrs Redhands hadn't only washed the curtains! She had washed the covers and the bedspreads, too. Those had to be ironed, and, dear me, what a long time they took!

"Now you hang up the curtains, Linnie, whilst I put everything away," said Mrs Redhands.

So poor Linnie had to get out the step-ladder and hang up all the clean curtains on their hooks. Dear me, she could hardly walk across the room when she had finished.

"Good!" said Mrs Redhands. "Now I really think everything is done. May I have my twenty-five pence please, Linnie?"

"Yes, here it is," said Linnie, giving the money to Mrs Redhands. "Thank you for your hard work."

"If you like I will come every week and give you a hand," said kind Mrs Redhands. "I can't bear to think of this little cottage getting all dirty again. We could easily do it together in one day – then if you want to be lazy for the rest of the week, you can."

"I'm *not* lazy!" cried Linnie crossly. "I'm not. And I'd rather you didn't come each week, Mrs Redhands, thank you. I can keep my cottage clean myself."

"Well, well – I'll just look in each Saturday morning and see how it's keeping," said Mrs Redhands, pinning on her hat. "Good night, Linnie."

Linnie sank down into her chair, quite tired out. "Oh dear, oh dear!" she sighed. "It's far harder work to have Mrs Redhands in than it would be to do the work myself each day! Good gracious me

- my legs are so tired that I can hardly get myself to bed!"

She did get to bed, and she fell fast asleep as once. And all night long she dreamt that she was working very hard indeed for Mrs Redhands.

When she woke up she looked round her clean, pretty bedroom and made a promise to herself.

"I won't have Mrs Redhands coming round every Saturday and making me work hard for her. I'll just work hard for myself each day. It won't be nearly so tiring!"

So that's what Linnie does now – and when Mrs Redhands pops her head in at the door on Saturday mornings she is always surprised to see such a spick-and-span cottage.

"Goodness gracious!" she says. "You *have* turned over a new leaf!"

And Linnie certainly has!

He Was
Sorry For Himself

"I've got a sore throat again," said Jeremy. He sat up in bed and swallowed. "Yes, I have. Oh dear, what a shame. I do feel sorry for myself. I'm a most unlucky boy."

He lay down again, and when his mother came in to tell him to get up and got to school he looked very miserable.

"I don't feel well," he said. "I've got a sore throat, Mother."

"Let's have a look," said his mother. He opened his mouth and she looked carefully at his throat.

"It's not very bad, Jeremy," she said. "Hardly a sore throat at all. But you had better not got to school. You can get up, and after breakfast you can go and play out in the sunshine. Your bicycle wants cleaning. You could make it nice and bright."

Jeremy didn't think Mother was making enough fuss of him. "I don't want to get up," he said. "I feel bad. I'm sure I'm going to be ill."

"No, you're not," said his mother impatiently. "You're just feeling sorry for yourself. Don't be silly now, Jeremy. I know you get a lot of colds and you have had a good deal of illness – but you let it get on top of you, and as soon as you begin to feel sorry for yourself you're no good at all! What about *you* getting on top of things for a change!"

"I can't," said Jeremy, looking very miserable. "I'm not strong enough."

"Oh, Jeremy!" said his mother, in despair. "I could be so proud of you, if only you would do your best instead of your worst! You have good brains and you could be top of your class. You're a lucky boy, because you have a nice home and a bicycle and an electric train and heaps of books. And, you know, if you really made up your mind you could soon forget your coughs and colds instead of lying here feeling so sorry for yourself."

She went out of the room. Jeremy lay

frowning in bed. Mother ought to be much sorrier for him! He was a most unlucky boy, *he* thought. He wasn't well and strong like the others were. He felt very sorry for himself indeed.

He did get up, because he had an idea that his mother would suddenly get cross with him. It was a beautiful day, so after breakfast he went out. "But it's not fair to make me work at cleaning my bicycle when I don't feel well," he said, and he tried to make his throat worse by coughing. Perhaps Mother would hear him and be sorry.

"Don't cough like that!" called Mother. "There's no need to and you'll only make your throat worse. And do cheer up, Jeremy. Your face is as long as a fiddle."

Jeremy felt cross then. He got on his bicycle. "I shall go for a long ride and not come back for ages," he thought. "Then Mother will wonder what has happened to me and she'll feel very sorry for me when I come back tired out."

He rode off. He pedalled down the road and up the hill. He free-wheeled down the

other side and then took a little lane he had never been down before. He would see where it led to.

It was a very long lane, and it wound in and out, in and out. Then it suddenly went into a long tunnel made of trees meeting overhead!

After a bit Jeremy got off his bicycle and sat down on the bank at one side. He was tired. He swallowed to see how his throat was. Dear, dear, it didn't feel any better at all! And he did believe his head was beginning to ache. He felt terribly sorry for

himself and gave an enormous sigh.

"Good gracious! What a wind you made then, sighing like that!" said a voice suddenly, and Jeremy jumped. A small, round man, not as big as Jeremy, dressed in red, was on the bank beside him.

Jeremy stared at him. What could this funny little man be?

"I'm a Reddy," said the little man. "You've heard of Brownies, I expect? Well, I'm a cousin of theirs, a Reddy. I live in that big tree just behind you, and I saw you when I came out of my front door."

This was all very surprising. Jeremy wondered if he could possibly be in a dream. He looked behind him at the big tree. He couldn't see any door at all. Ivy grew over the trunk and hid the bark just there.

"The ivy hides my door," said the Reddy. "Won't you come in and sit down for a bit? I suppose you're tired, as you sighed like that."

"Yes," said Jeremy, and sighed again. "And my throat is sore, and I do believe I've got a headache coming. I really ought to be in bed. But my mother sent me out."

"Poor, poor boy," said the Reddy. "Well, do come in. I've got one or two friends coming for a glass of lemonade. You might like one – unless your throat is too sore for you to swallow?"

"Oh, it's all right for swallowing lemonade," said Jeremy.

The little man lifted up a little curtain of ivy, and there behind it was the neatest front door you ever saw. The Reddy fitted a key into the lock and swung it open. Jeremy went inside. There was a perfectly round room there. It was strange inside

the tree, because it looked much bigger there than it had looked outside. A bench ran all round, and on it were sitting two other Reddies, one with a bright red beard that he wore round his neck just like a scarf.

"Hallo, who's this?" said one Reddy.

"A poor little boy who's tired, and who's got a sore throat, and thinks he's going to have a headache," said the first Reddy. "And his mother's sent him out instead of keeping him in bed."

The Reddy with the beard looked hard at Jeremy. "I know this boy," he said. "I live at the bottom of his garden. He's the boy I've often told you about – the one who's always so sorry for himself."

"Oh – is *that* the boy?" said the other Reddies and they stared at Jeremy. The bearded Reddy nodded.

"Yes. He loves being sorry for himself. Don't you, Jeremy? Really, he's an awfully lucky boy. He's got a nice home, and a lovely mother and a fine father, and a big garden to play in, and a bicycle and all kinds of toys. But if he were an *unlucky* boy, he could be really and truly very, *very* sorry for himself, couldn't he?"

"Yes. That would be nice for him," said the first Reddy. "If he loves being sorry for himself he'd better have some bad luck."

Jeremy began to feel rather alarmed. He drank some of the very sweet lemonade that the first Reddy had poured out for him.

"I don't think ..." began Jeremy. But the Reddies went on talking as if he wasn't there.

"You know," said the bearded one, undoing his beard and then tying it more tightly round his neck again, "you know I can't quite make out why he's so terribly sorry for himself always. Certainly he's had a fair amount of illness – but then lots of children have. He makes himself much worse by giving in to it and feeling so sorry. That shows how much he enjoys feeling upset about himself."

"Yes, it does," said the others, and they drank their lemonade, looking rather solemn. "Can't we help him a bit – give him more things to feel sorry about? He'd enjoy that. Think how he'd grumble and moan if we took his mother away for a bit, for instance, and made him hurt his leg badly, and had his bicycle stolen. He *would* feel sorry for himself then!"

Jeremy felt more alarmed than ever. He put down his glass. "Look here," he said, "I don't like you to talk like this. I can't help always having something wrong with me, can I? I don't make my colds come!"

"That's true," said the bearded Reddy. "But you make things much worse by

being so sorry for yourself instead of squaring your shoulders and saying: 'What! Something wrong with me! I'll soon deal with *that!*' You act like a little coward instead of a brave boy with brains and plenty of things to be thankful for!"

"You're horrid!" said Jeremy, and he dashed out of the door. He slammed it hard. "I won't stay there a minute more!" he thought. "I'll ride straight home and tell Mother!"

But his bicycle was gone! It simply wasn't there. Jeremy hunted up and down the lane for it, but it was gone.

"It's been stolen!" he wailed. "Oh, those

hateful Reddies. *They've* done this! Oh, what an unlucky boy I am!"

A little voice called out mockingly from the hedge: "Are you enjoying feeling sorry for yourself, Jeremy? You'll soon feel sorrier still!"

Jeremy stamped his foot. "You be quiet!" he shouted.

There was the sound of a laugh and then of a door being slammed. Jeremy stamped

his foot again. He felt like crying. But he wasn't going to! Those Reddies would be pleased if they saw him crying and being sorry for himself.

"I'm going to walk all the way home and *enjoy* it," he shouted, and off he went down the lane. He walked and he walked. It took him a long, long time to get home, and he really did feel tired when he got there.

And, oh dear, when he went in at the garden door Sarah, the daily help, called out bad news to him.

"Is that you, Jeremy? Your mother has heard that your father has had an accident and she's had to go to see him."

"Oh," said Jeremy, his heart sinking into his boots. That was those Reddies again – trying to make him feel more and more sorry for himself. Well, he wouldn't! He'd feel sorry for his mother and father instead.

"Your poor mother left in such a hurry," said Sarah, coming in with his dinner. "She was in the middle of turning out that cupboard there – and she meant to have tidied out the garage to save your father doing it at the weekend. She left you a message and said if your throat was any worse you'd better go to bed."

"I'm *not* going to bed," said Jeremy, and he squared his shoulders and spoke in a loud voice. "I'm going to finish turning out that cupboard for Mother – and I'm going to tidy the garage too. I know exactly what to do because Mother told me what she had planned to do there."

"But you look tired, Jeremy," said Sarah.

"I am," said Jeremy, "because my bicycle has been stolen and I had to walk back. But you needn't think I'm sorry for myself. I'm just thinking of Mother and Daddy, and I want to do something for them."

Jeremy felt very guilty, because he couldn't help thinking that all this bad luck had happened just because the Reddies wanted him to feel even sorrier for himself than before. But he wasn't going to think of himself at all. He'd show them! He'd think of Mother and Daddy and work hard all day to make up to them for this bad luck.

He did. He forgot his sore throat, and it went. He didn't have a headache after all. His legs ached, but he didn't bother about that. He turned out the cupboard. He tidied the garage beautifully. He cleaned his mother's bicycle, and he swept the kitchen yard for Sarah.

"I never knew what a nice boy you could be!" said Sarah. "I always thought you were a poor little thing that couldn't pull yourself together at all and just waited for bad things to happen to you. My, Jeremy, you look different today – sort of determined and strong."

"And so I am!" said Jeremy, and he set the brush down with a bang. "And if

anybody in this house ever dares to say I'm the sort of boy that's always sorry for himself I'll tell them what I think of them!"

He stalked away into the hall, leaving Sarah staring after him in surprise. Well, well – she'd thought that Jeremy would come whining home and go to bed and burst into tears when he heard the news. But here he was, behaving like a hero!

A taxi drew up at the door. Jeremy rushed to the front, his heart beating fast. Was his father badly hurt? Would his mother be terribly upset?

His mother got out first and then turned to help his father out. He was limping, but he didn't look at all ill. "Hallo, Jeremy!" he called. "I hope you didn't think I'd been run over or anything! I just fell down the office stairs and sprained my ankle – but I'll be all right in a few days!"

Jeremy heaved a sigh of relief. So it wasn't the dreadful bad luck he had been fearing after all. It was hardly bad at all!

"How are you, Jeremy dear?" asked his mother anxiously.

"Fine!" said Jeremy, and he squared his shoulders and looked sturdy and tall. "Nothing wrong with me at all! I've been working hard for you all day!"

His mother was delighted. His father was pleased, too. He put his arm round Jeremy and spoke to him in a warm, friendly voice.

"You know, son," he said, "when I slipped and fell today, I thought, 'My goodness, suppose I was killed! I can't trust Jeremy to look after his mother, because he's always so sorry for himself.' And I was worried. But now I see I've got a good little son and I'm glad."

"Yes," said Jeremy, stoutly, "you can count on me now, Daddy."

And did he mean what he said? Yes, of course he did!

Polly's
P's and Q's

Have you ever heard anyone say to a boy or girl, "Now just mind your P's and Q's?"

Well, Polly was a little girl who *didn't* mind hers! She was always forgetting her pleases and thank yous. The P's are the pleases you see, and the Q's are the thank yous. If you say, "Thank you," you will hear the Q at the end!

"Will you have some more pudding?" Polly's mother would say. And Polly would answer, "Yes."

"Yes, what?" her mother would say. *"How* many times must I tell you to say *Please?* It does sound so rude to say 'Yes' like that. You should say, 'Yes, please, Mummy'."

Then she would give Polly her pudding, and the little girl would take it – and forget to say "Thank you!"

She really was dreadful!

One day her Aunt Jessica came to tea. Polly was a bit afraid of her, because she was rather strict and she always said that Polly was spoilt.

Aunt Jessica brought out a packet of butterscotch. She nearly always had some sweets in her bag. She offered some to Mummy. "Thank you, Jessica," said Mummy, and took a piece.

"Would you like some butterscotch too, Polly?" asked Aunt Jessica.

"Yes," said Polly at once. She loved butterscotch. Aunt Jessica glared. "I'll

give you another chance, Polly," she said crossly. "Would you like to have a piece of my butterscotch?"

"Yes," said Polly. She didn't think of saying "Please," you see!

"No pleases today, I see," said Aunt Jessica, putting away her packet of sweets. "Well – no pleases, no butterscotch!"

"Please!" said Polly. Aunt Jessica looked very cross still, but she undid the packet and offered it to Polly. Polly took a piece and began to unwrap the paper.

But Aunt Jessica put out her hand and took the butterscotch from her. She wrapped it up again and put it into the packet.

"You bad-mannered little girl!" she said. "Not even a thank you now!"

"Oh, thank you!" cried Polly. But it was too late this time. Aunt Jessica put the butterscotch away in her bag. She turned to Mummy.

"Alice, I can't *think* why you don't teach Polly her manners!" she said. "I'm really ashamed of my niece. What *must* people think of her when she goes out to tea and never says *Please* or *Thank you?*"

"I don't know," said Mummy, looking worried. "I do try to teach her, Jessica – I really do. But she forgets so often. I really do *not* know what to do! Could *you* tell me what to do? You're so clever with children."

"Dear me, yes, I can tell you what to do," said Aunt Jessica at once. "Every time she forgets her P's and Q's pin one on to her – she won't like being hung with them, I am sure – and they will remind her of what she keeps forgetting."

"Well, that's a good idea," said Mummy with a laugh, and she began to cut out lots of letter P's and Q's from some white cotton stuff. When she had about thirty,

70

she stuck a safety-pin into each one.

"There!" she said. "They're all ready! Polly, here are your P's and Q's. Every time you remember one, it shall go into the waste-paper basket. But every time you forget one, it shall come to you!"

Polly thought it was a horrid idea. She made up her mind she wouldn't have a single one of the nasty letters pinned to her. She sat looking sulky.

71

Aunt Jessica and Mummy went on talking about something else. Polly's gran came into the room with a rosy apple. "Would you like an apple, Polly?" she asked.

"Yes!" shouted Polly, and she ran to take it. She didn't say "Please," and she didn't say "Thank you"! Aunt Jessica at once took up a large white P and a large white Q from the table.

"Come here, Polly," she said. Polly went to her slowly. Aunt Jessica pinned the P on to the front of her jersey, and the Q on to her skirt.

"There!" she said. "There's the Please you forgot and the Thank you you forgot. They have both come to live with you!"

Polly was ashamed, but do you know, she had got into such a bad habit of forgetting her P's and Q's that she forgot them three times before Aunt Jessica went home! So she had three more P's and three more Q's pinned on to her, back and front, before bedtime came.

"Can I take them off now?" asked Polly, when she undressed.

"Oh no," said Gran. "Mummy says you

must keep them on till you remember. It will be strange for you to put on your jersey and skirt tomorrow, with all these funny white letters on. I do think you are silly not to remember your P's and Q's. Other children do."

Well, Polly didn't at all like putting on her skirt and jersey next morning, with so many white letters pinned there. She was glad that Daddy had gone to town before he saw her. He *would* have laughed at her!

At breakfast-time Mummy said to Polly,

73

"Would you like sugar or treacle with your porridge this morning, Polly?"

"Treacle," said Polly – and then she suddenly remembered! "Treacle, PLEASE, Mummy!" she said.

"Good girl," said Mummy. "I will unpin one of the P's. Come here." So one of the horrid P's was taken away and thrown into the waste-paper basket. Polly was glad. "Oh, I'll soon get rid of them all!" she thought.

But it wasn't so easy. She twice forgot to say *Please* to Gran, and three times forgot a *Thank you*. So Gran had to pin five more letters on her. And Mummy pinned seven more, by the end of the morning. Wasn't it dreadful!

"Well, this just shows you what bad manners you have, Polly," said Mummy sadly. "I can hardly believe you forget so much!"

That afternoon Alan came to ask if Polly could go home to tea with him. "Can I, Mummy, PLEASE?" asked Polly.

Mummy unpinned a P and threw it away. "Yes, you may go," she said. "But dear me, *I* shouldn't like to go all pinned up with P's and Q's!"

"Oh!" cried Polly in dismay. "Must I take them with me?"

"Certainly," said Mummy. "You've got to get rid of them by remembering them."

"Then I shan't go out to tea," said Polly, and she began to cry, because Alan was laughing at her skirt, all pinned over with white letters.

So she didn't go out to tea, and she was very sad indeed. She sat in a corner and cried. Gran was sorry for her.

"Cheer up, Polly," she said. "You know quite well that you can get rid of *all* those letters if you really try. You only need to think hard when you answer anybody.

Cheer up, do! Shall I read to you for a while?"

"Yes, Gran, PLEASE!" said Polly at once. Gran unpinned a P. She took down a book and Polly got on her knee.

"Thank you, Gran!" said Polly. Off came another Q! Good!

When Gran had finished the story, Polly spoke to her. "PLEASE, Gran, will you read another?"

Off came another P. This was fine. When the story was finished, Polly said, "Thank you, Gran, I loved that."

Off went a Q. Gran was surprised and glad. "Well, you really do sound perfectly sweet when you speak like that," she told Polly. "Good-mannered children are always nice to be with, and it's a pleasure to hear you talk so politely."

You will hardly believe it, but before that day was done, Polly had had every single P and Q unpinned from her skirt! Not one was left. They were all in the waste-paper basket!

"I wonder if I ought to cut some more for tomorrow!" said Mummy. "I'd better, I think."

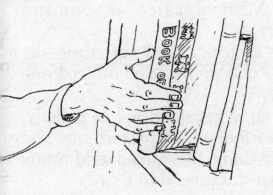

"No, Mummy, THANK YOU!" said Polly at once. "I'm always going to remember now."

"Well, I hope you do," said Mummy, "because Aunt Jessica is coming again tomorrow."

She came as usual, and this time she had a box of chocolates. She offered one to Polly.

"Thank you, Aunt Jessica," said Polly. Aunt Jessica looked surprised, but she didn't say anything. She talked to Mummy for a bit, then she turned to Polly.

"Would you like to show me your garden?" she asked.

"Yes, please, Aunt Jessica," said Polly, jumping up, pleased to show her pretty garden.

"Bless us all!" said Aunt Jessica, staring in astonishment at Polly. "How did she learn such nice manners all of a sudden? Don't tell me it was the P's and Q's!"

"It was, Jessica," said Mummy, laughing. "You should have seen Polly yesterday morning – covered with P's and Q's from head to foot. She *did* look silly. But she suddenly made up her mind she couldn't bear it, and before she went to bed she had got rid of them all, and had learnt the nicest way of speaking you can imagine!"

"Splendid!" said Aunt Jessica, and she gave Polly a hug. "You're a nice little girl, my dear, but even the nicest people can be spoilt if they have bad manners. I shall be proud of you now, I'm sure!"

She is, because Polly didn't once have another P or Q pinned to her. Everyone likes to have her to tea because she has such nice manners. It was a funny way of learning her P's and Q's, wasn't it? I do hope you'll never have to learn in Polly's way – but I'm sure you won't!

On His
Way Home

"That's all for tonight," said the choir-master. "Richard, you sang better than ever. You've got more music in you than all the others here put together! I wish you could give them a little!"

Richard didn't even hear what the choir-master said. He was dreaming as usual, thinking out the tunes *he* could put to some of the carols they had been practising for Christmas week.

"Richard's dreaming of the time when he's grown-up and sings at concerts all over the world and makes more money than he'll know what to do with!" said one of the boys, who was jealous of Richard.

The choir-master looked at the dreamy Richard. He was certain that the boy would become famous when he grew up. He lived for his music and his singing, and

what was more, he worked hard at it too.

"Yes," he said, "Richard will be richer than any of us. He won't be able to help it. But let's hope he'll think of others besides himself when success and wealth come to him!"

Richard was the last to go home. He always was because he was slow and didn't think what he was doing. But at last he went out of the church, and looked up into the frosty sky, full of stars.

As he turned a corner, he heard the sound of a violin, and he stopped. It was a cheap violin – but how beautifully it was

being played. The player spoilt it, though, by trying to sing to the melody.

Richard looked at him. He was an old and dirty fellow, with straggly grey hair, and stained, ragged clothes. His voice was hoarse and cracked as he tried to sing the lovely old carols. People laughed at him. Two boys sent a stone skimming down the road at him. No one threw money in the shabby hat put down at the man's feet.

"What a horrible noise!" said people passing by. "We would give him money to go away, but none for his dreadful singing!"

Richard was struck by the man's playing. A poor, cheap violin – but how marvellously played. He went up to the man.

"I like the way you play," he said. "You play wonderfully!"

The old man took his bow from the strings and peered at the boy. "I once had a famous name," he said. "I played all over Europe. Now I'm a poor old beggar-man scraping a cheap violin – and I can't earn anything for a meal, nothing for a bit of fire, or a warm coat. But it's done me good to have a boy come and tell me I can still play! Can you play too?"

"I can sing," said Richard. "I'll sing to your violin, if you like. Play the tunes of the old carols and I'll sing for you. Perhaps you'll get some money if I sing and you play."

The old man put his violin under his chin again. The first few notes of "Silent Night" came stealing on the night-air.

Richard lifted his head. "Silent night, Holy night," he sang, his voice as pure as an angel's.

The old man stared in amazement and delight – what a voice! Ah, this boy was a pleasure to play for. Violin and voice mingled, and people passing by stopped suddenly. Who was this singing? Who

was it playing? Two masters of music, surely! But under the light of the lamp-post they saw only a young boy and an old and dirty beggar.

A little crowd gathered round, listening in silence. The choir-master came by on his way home, astonished by the voice, unable to believe it could be Richard's. The carol came to an end. A stream of coins poured into the hat. Richard looked down at the old hat in delight. What a lot of money!

The beggar ran his bow gently over the strings again. "Noel! Noel!" sang the strings, and Richard's voice joined in, clear and lovely to hear in the dark, frosty night.

The crowd joined in at the end of each

verse, and once more the money rained down into the old hat. Then a policeman loomed up apologetically.

"Sorry – but you must move on," he said. The crowd sighed. What a pity! They had never heard carols they enjoyed more. Richard picked up the heavy hat and gave it to the old man.

"There must be enough here to buy you all you want this Christmas week!" he said. "I'm glad."

"Take half," said the beggar, but Richard pushed the hat away.

"No. I couldn't take money for singing

to your lovely playing. You have it all."
The boy ran home, humming a carol tune
under his breath. The old man looked
after him and the choir-master heard him
muttering to himself.

"Ah, you'll be a great musician one
day, my boy – and you'll be a great man
too! You won't only think of your music –
you'll think of your fellow-men." And off
went the old man with his pockets full of
money – the first money that Richard had
ever earned.

Good luck to you, Richard. You've begun
the right way.

The
Broken Gate

Old Man Twinkle wanted a boy to help him in his shop. He needed a boy who could drive Jenny, the pony, for all Twinkle's goods were taken round in the cart.

So Old Man Twinkle put a notice in his window: "WANTED – BOY TO HELP (After School Hours)."

All the boys saw the notice and many of them thought they would try for the job. They could do it after school, and on Saturdays, and it would be a good job, for Old Man Twinkle was generous and kind.

"It means good food, good pocket-money, and great fun driving Jenny round to deliver the goods," said George. "I'm going after that job!"

"So am I," said Henry. "My mother could do with a bit of extra money and so could I."

"And I'd love to drive old Jenny," said Peter. "I could give you all rides."

"You're not allowed to do that," said Jack, the smallest. "Old Man Twinkle always says that Jenny has enough to pull without taking on extra passengers."

"Pooh! I don't care what Old Man Twinkle says," said Harry. "If *I* got the job I'd do the same as Peter – give you all a ride if I met you!"

WANTED
BOY TO HELP
(after school hrs)
APPLY WITHI

"Shall you try for the job too, Jack?" asked George.

"No! What good would I be?" said Jack. "I'm too small – and look at my clothes! I don't look good enough to go after a job."

"I bet *I*'ll get it," said George. "I'm the biggest of you all!"

"Well, I'm top of the class, so my brains ought to get it for *me!*" said Henry.

"And I *look* the best," said Harry, smoothing down his new suit. He was always nicely dressed and neat.

"My father knows Old Man Twinkle well," said Peter. "I guess I'll get the job because Twinkle likes my father."

"Well, we'll see," said George. "It's a pity Jack can't try for the job too – but he's so small, and not a bit strong, and he does look rather ragged. I wonder which of us will get it. Hope I do! I'd like a good meal every evening and money in my pocket – and shouldn't I feel great trotting along with Jenny the pony!"

That evening all the boys went to see Old Man Twinkle. Jack went too, to see who would get the job. Old Man Twinkle wasn't ready to see anyone for the moment, so he told the boys to play in the yard till he called them.

"I say! Let's have a swing on that gate!" said Harry, seeing an enormous yard-gate swinging to and fro in the wind. "Come on – let's get up on it and pretend we are riding a horse!"

All five boys climbed up on to the gate. They shouted and pretended to whip the gate to make it gallop. It swung to and fro, and the boys shouted with delight.

And then suddenly something happened. The gate was old and was not meant to carry five heavy boys! It broke away at the hinges, and the boys found themselves sliding off! The gate gave a groan and hung all crooked, swinging in a very peculiar manner.

"I say! We've broken the gate!" said Harry in a small voice.

"What will Old Man Twinkle say?" asked Peter. "He will be angry!"

"Don't let's tell him," said George. "He's at the front of the shop. He can't see what's happened."

"But we *ought* to tell him," said Jack. "It's rather cowardly not to. My mother says we always ought to own up at once when anything's broken. Can't we all five go and tell him?"

"No," said Henry. "He might say he won't give any of us the job if we've done a thing like that. We won't say a word."

"Right," said Harry, "Look – Old Man Twinkle is shouting to us. I'll go first."

He went to see the old man. Twinkle

asked him some questions, and at the end he suddenly said, "Do you know anything about that broken gate?"

"Er – is it broken, sir?" said Harry, pretending to be surprised.

"Yes, it is," said Twinkle, rather sharply. "You can go now. Send in the next boy."

Peter came in, and Twinkle asked him the same sort of questions that he had asked Harry. And at the end he suddenly shot the same question at him, "Do you know anything about that broken gate?"

"Oh no, sir!" said Peter untruthfully.

"You may go," said Twinkle. "Send in the next boy. I'll make my choice when I've seen you all."

George came in, and after a while Twinkle asked him the same question, "Do you know anything about that broken gate?"

"It was broken when we came in, sir," said George most untruthfully, and he blushed red, for he knew he should never tell stories like that.

"Really?" said Twinkle, and he frowned. "You may go. Send in the next boy."

Henry came in, and he had the same

question asked him at the end, "Do you know anything about that broken gate?"

"*I* didn't break it, sir," said Henry.

"Are you sure you didn't?" asked Twinkle.

"Quite sure," said Henry.

"You may go," said Twinkle. "Send in the next boy."

"I'm the last," said Henry. "And please, sir, I'm the top of my class and my master says I've got good brains. I'm sure I'd do well for you, sir."

"I'll make my choice this evening

sometime," said Twinkle. "It's not only cleverness I want. It's something bigger."

"And what's that, sir?" asked Henry. But Twinkle waved him out, and he went to join the others.

"He'll make his choice sometime this evening," said Henry. "We'd better go home and wait and see who it is. Come on."

They all went off – except Jack. He was worried about the broken gate. It was dreadful to break a thing and not to tell about it – and not even try and mend it. He wondered if he *could* mend it. He swung the gate a little to see

how much it was broken.

Old Man Twinkle saw Jack from the window. He called him in. "Are you another boy after this job?" he asked.

"No, sir," said Jack. "I'm too small and not very clever – and I'm a bit ragged, too, because my mother hasn't much money."

"Hm!" said Old Man Twinkle. "I see. Well, what are you doing out there in my yard? Do you know anything about that broken gate?"

"Oh dear!" thought Jack. "Now what am I to say? I don't want to get the other boys into trouble!"

He went red – and then he said, "Yes,

Mr Twinkle, I do know about that gate."

"What do you know about it?" asked Old Man Twinkle.

"I was swinging on it when it broke," said Jack bravely, though he didn't feel at all brave, for Twinkle was frowning.

"Oh! So your weight broke my gate did it?" said Old Man Twinkle, and he looked fierce.

"Well – not exactly," said Jack.

"What do you mean – not exactly?" asked Twinkle.

"Oh, please, sir, don't be angry, but you see, some other boys and I were all

swinging together on it, and it broke," said Jack. "I wanted to come and tell you, really I did. But the others said no, and I couldn't give them away, could I? I stayed to see if I could mend the gate. That's what I was doing out in the yard."

"I see," said Old Man Twinkle, and he didn't look quite so fierce now. "Well – who were the other boys?"

"Don't be angry with me, Mr Twinkle, but I really can't tell tales," said poor Jack. "They are my friends, you see, and I don't want them to get into trouble."

"Quite so," said Old Man Twinkle. "And now I am going to tell *you* something. The boy's names were Harry, Peter, George, and Henry! You see – I know them all!"

Jack stared in surprise. "How did you know?" he asked. "Did the boys tell you after all?"

"Not one of them," said Old Man Twinkle. "They pretended to be surprised. They pretended not to know. They told me untruths. But I happened to see you all swinging on the gate when it broke. So I knew all about it, you see."

"Oh," said Jack, and he stared at Mr

Twinkle again. "Well, please choose one of the boys," he said. "They are nice boys, really – although they didn't own up about the gate."

"I've chosen my boy," said Mr Twinkle.

"Who is he?" asked Jack.

"He is *you!*" said Mr Twinkle. "Yes, I know you are small – but you'll grow, especially if Mrs Twinkle makes you pudding every night. And I know you're at the bottom of the class for lots of things – but good food will make your brains grow too! And I know you're a bit ragged – but a little pocket-money will buy you better clothes!"

"Oh, Mr Twinkle!" cried Jack. "But – but – why do you choose a boy like me? The others are bigger and cleverer."

"They may be," said Mr Twinkle. "But what I want is a boy who is brave enough to own up when things go wrong. I want a boy who can speak the truth. I want a boy who is loyal – and if you are loyal to your friends, as you have been just now, you'll be loyal to me too! I've chosen the right boy, Jack – ah, I've chosen the right boy!"

So he had, for Jack is with him still –

but not as errand-boy. Oh no – he is the head of the shop now, and doing very well indeed. All because of a broken gate – wasn't it strange?

Sulky Susan

Susan was a sulky little girl. You know what sulky means, don't you? It's when you are cross and won't smile or talk nicely and your mouth turns down instead of up.

Well, Susan was nearly always like that. Everyone called her Sulky Susan. "Susan's in the sulks again!" her friends said, when they saw her mouth turning down. "Look at her! Poor old Susan!"

One day an old man met Susan running down the lane. She didn't look where she was going and she bumped into him, bang! He was quite astonished, and so was Susan.

"Little girl, you should really look where you are going," said the old man. "You might have hurt yourself and me too."

Now any other child would have said, "Oh, I'm so sorry. I'll look next time."

But not Susan! Oh no! She didn't say a word, but just went into one of her sulks.

She stared up at the old man, her mouth sulky and her forehead one big frown.

"Bless us all!" said the old man, laughing. "Where did you get that dreadful face, little girl?"

That made Susan sulk even more – and then she saw something that made her heart begin to beat rather fast.

The old man had pointed ears – and behind his glasses his eyes shone green. Susan knew enough fairy-tales to know that this old man wasn't an ordinary

fellow. No, he must belong to the fairy folk.

She had better be careful!

She was just going to run away when the old man took her arm.

She tried to wriggle off but it was no use. "Now I'd just like you to meet someone," he said in a very pleasant voice. "Come along. She lives not far away."

Susan had to go with him. He turned down a funny crooked street that Susan had never seen before and knocked on the door of a house. A girl about fourteen years old opened the door.

Susan thought she had a most unpleasant face. She frowned at them, and spoke in a sharp voice.

"What do you want?"

"Only to see you for a moment," said the old man. "Susan dear – this is Susan Hill, aged fourteen. Do you like her?"

Now Susan Hill was Susan's own name. Wasn't it strange? Susan stared at the big girl and thought she was simply horrid. She looked so very cross. She had pretty hair, golden like Susan's, and a dimple in her chin too, just like Susan's. Her nose

was larger than Susan's but it was just the same shape. In fact, she might have been Susan's bigger sister.

"Well, if you have finished staring at me I'll shut the door," said Susan Hill in a cross voice, and she slammed the door hard. The old man turned to Susan. "Did you like her?" he asked.

"Not a bit," said Susan, still sulking.

"Well, there's someone else I'd like you to meet, too," said the old man, and he took Susan down another street. He called to a young woman who was hanging out clothes in a garden. She was about twenty-one, and from the back she looked pretty and young, for she had fine yellow hair that was like a golden mist round her head.

The old man called to her. "Come and meet a little friend of mine."

The young woman turned – and what a shock Susan got. She wasn't at all pretty from the front, because her face was so sulky and cross. Her mouth turned down and she had three wrinkles across her pretty forehead.

"This young woman is called Susan

106

Hill," said the old man to little Susan. "Shake hands."

"I haven't time to waste bothering with children!" said the young woman crossly. "I've all these things to peg up on the line." Susan stared at the cross young woman, puzzled. She was so like the young girl she had seen, but older – and her name was Susan Hill, too. How funny!

"Do you like her?" asked the old man.

"No," said Susan. "She's so cross-looking. I thought she was going to be so pretty and nice from the back, but from the front she was horrid."

"You're right," said the old man.

"There seem to be a lot of people living about here with the same name as mine," said Susan. "Are there any more?"

"I can show you two more if you like," said the old man. "Look, here comes one!"

Down the street came a rather fat and ugly woman. She would not have been so ugly if only she had smiled, because her hair was so pretty and soft round her face, and there was a dimple in her chin that could have gone in and out when she smiled. But she really was a most unpleasant woman, for she had lines from her nose to her chin, her mouth was turned right down, and she frowned all the time. Susan thought she was horrid.

"It's funny that none of the Susan Hills are married," she said.

"Not so very funny really," said the old man. "Nobody likes sulky people, or unkind people, do they? So why should anyone want to marry them? *I* wouldn't."

Susan began to feel a little uncomfortable. She thought that all this was very strange indeed. She wished she could go home.

"Where is the other Susan Hill?" she asked, after they had walked a good way.

"There she is, coming along tap-tap-tapping with a stick!" said the old man. Susan looked – and, dear me, she nearly ran away in alarm! A most cross-looking old dame was coming along the road. Her face was thin and wrinkled, her mouth was cross, her eyes had almost disappeared under the wrinkles that had come with frowning.

"That's Susan Hill," said the old man. "How do you like yourself all through your life, Susan? It is yourself you have been looking at, you know … Susan Hill, aged 14. Susan Hill aged 21. Susan Hill aged 45,

and Susan Hill aged 70. Do you think you will like to be her?"

Susan stared at the old man in horror. "It can't be me!" she cried. "It can't! Oh, don't let me be like that!"

"*I* can't help you, my child," said the old man. "You can only help yourself. You have the prettiest golden hair that is meant to frame a smiling face. You have blue eyes that should twinkle, and a pretty mouth that should turn up and not down. And you have a dimple in your chin that should always be there, all your life. You make your own face, you know. Look at yours in the glass and see what it is like now!"

Susan looked up at the old man's green eyes, twinkling behind his glasses – and then a very strange thing happened. She wasn't looking into those green eyes – she was looking into her own eyes! She was in her own bedroom, looking into her own little mirror.

She saw her sulky face. She saw her eyes drooping at the corners. She saw her cross mouth turning down. She saw a very ugly little girl. "Now let's see the difference

when I smile!" said Susan to herself. So she smiled into the glass.

And the ugly child turned into a pretty one at once! The blue eyes lighted up and shone. The dimple danced in and out. The frown went. The mouth curved upwards and showed Susan's pretty white teeth.

"It's like magic!" thought Susan. "Just like magic. My own magic. That old man said I could make my own face – and I *will* make it too! I'll make it sweet and smiling, happy and pretty – not like those dreadful Susan Hills he showed me. And I'll begin from this very, very minute!"

So downstairs danced Susan, smiling

all over her face. Her mother was too surprised to speak for a moment. Then she cried out in pleasure.

"What's happened to you, child? I've never seen you look so sweet before!"

Well – I saw Susan yesterday, and she's a darling, with her twinkling eyes and her upturned mouth. And she'll still be a darling, no matter how old she grows. I hope you will, too! Go and look into the mirror when you are wearing a sulky face – and smile at yourself.

You *will* be astonished at the magical change!

John's Hanky

It was very very hot. Mother told the two children that they really must put on their sun-hats when they went to play in the garden.

After dinner they sat on the hot garden-seat with their books. Alice had on her sun-hat. John had forgotten his, and he felt the sun burning his head.

"Bother!" he said to himself. "I don't want to have to go all the way to the house to fetch my hat. I know what I'll do. I'll knot my hanky at each corner and make a nice little sun-cap of it."

So he took out his big hanky from his pocket, and knotted it carefully in each corner. Then he set it on his head and took up his book to read.

His bookmark blew into the rose-bushes after a bit, and John got up to get it. He scratched his hand badly on a rose-thorn and gave a yell.

"Ooooh! Look at that! It's bleeding like anything! I must bind it up at once."

He put his hand into his pocket to get out his hanky. But it wasn't there, of course. He put his hand into his shirt, but he hadn't tucked it there either. He looked on the seat and on the ground. No hanky.

"Don't fidget," said Alice. "I'm reading."

"Lend me your hanky then. I've hurt my hand," said John.

Alice looked at him. Then she laughed. "Use your own!" she said.

"I haven't got it," said John, crossly.

"Yes, you have," said Alice.

"No, I haven't," said John. "You tell me where it is, if you think I have got it with me."

"Shan't!" said Alice, and laughed again. Then John got cross and pushed her. She fell off the seat and yelled. She grabbed John by the knees and he fell off the seat too.

Soon they were rolling over and over on the grass, shouting and shoving each other.

At last John sat hard on Alice.

"Now you tell me where my hanky is!" he said. "Or I'll sit on you even harder. Have you taken it?"

"No! It's on your head, silly!" said Alice, and began to laugh again. Oh dear – so it was. John did feel foolish. He went indoors and got his sun-hat then!

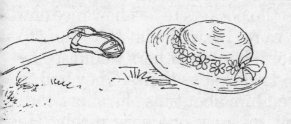

He
Was Afraid!

Alan had a new jacket. He was pleased with it because his old one had been much too short for him, and one of its sleeves had a patch over the elbow.

"Now you really look very nice in this new jacket," his mother said to him. "I feel proud of you in it! You look quite grown up. You will remember not to wear it except for going to school, or going out to tea, won't you? You mustn't wear it when you go out to play, or else it will get dirty and torn."

"I promise!" said Alan, and put his hands into the pockets to feel how nice and deep they were. He wished it were time to go to school. Then the others would see he had as good a jacket as theirs. They had so often teased him about his old, short one.

He kept his new one very nicely. He

always hung it up on its peg at school. He hung it up as soon as he got home, too, instead of flinging it down anywhere. His mother was pleased with him.

"You're really growing up, when you begin to take care of things," she told Alan. "That jacket is as nice now, after you've had it a month, as it was when I first tried it on you. Daddy's pleased about it too. He says if you're really learning to take care

117

of your things he might give you a bicycle for your birthday, after all. He's always said no till now, because he was sure you wouldn't take care of it."

"Oh – I'd love a bicycle!" said Alan, his face one big smile. "Oh, Mother do, do let me have one."

Now, a week after this, Alan's friend, Peter, asked him to go and play with him on a Saturday morning. "Take the short cut across the field," he said. "You get to our farm quicker that way."

So, when Saturday morning came, Alan went to get his cap and jacket and scarf. He thought he had better put on his wellingtons, too, because it had been raining hard and everywhere was muddy.

He looked into the cupboard where the jackets were kept. There were his two, the new one and the old one. He put his hand to take down his old one.

Then he frowned. "No, I can't wear that. It's shorter than ever now I've grown a bit. It's all right to play in at home in the garden, but I really can't go to Peter's in it. Peter's mother would think I looked dreadful."

Alan's mother was out shopping. Then she was going to see Granny. She wouldn't be back till Alan was home again from Peter's. So she wouldn't know which jacket he put on.

Alan pulled down his new jacket and put it on quickly. Then on went scarf, cap and wellingtons, and he was ready.

Out he went, and ran all the way to Peter's. Peter was waiting for him. "Hallo! My mother says it's too muddy to play out-of-doors, so let's go in and get out my trains," he said.

Peter's mother was out, so Alan needn't have worried about which jacket to put on, after all! He hung his jacket up in the hall,

and went to play with Peter. "I've got to leave at twelve o'clock," he said. "Don't let me forget!"

"Right. And when you go, take the path up by the pig-sties," said Peter. "There are some tiny piglets there, the funniest little things you ever saw."

So, when Alan said goodbye, he took the path up to the pig-sties. In one of them were eight little piglets, running about making funny noises. Alan thought they were very comical indeed. He climbed over the gate and went into the sty to play with the piglets.

But something suddenly got up out of the mud and charged at him with a fearful grunt! It was the old mother-sow. She had been lying down quietly at the far end, and Alan hadn't even noticed her, because she was so dirty with mud.

Alan turned to run to the gate, but the sow ran right into him before he got there. He fell on his face in the mud. Two of the piglets ran over him in delight. The sow nosed him, and grunted loudly.

Alan got up, and the sow immediately knocked him over again. This time he

rolled on his back. He shouted tearfully at the great animal: "Go away! I wasn't doing any harm. Stop running at me!"

The sow waited till he had got up once more and then ran at him again. But this time Alan managed to get to the gate before he was knocked over. He scrambled over and caught his jacket on a nail. There was a tearing sound – and when he looked down, he saw a large hole in it.

Soon he was running home, trying not to cry. He looked at his jacket. It was covered

with mud, and torn down the front. And it was his new jacket!

Alan stopped running. He felt frightened. What would his mother say? She had told him not to wear his new jacket when he went out to play. Now look at it! She would be so angry that she would tell his father, and he certainly wouldn't get him a bicycle for his birthday.

Alan's heart sank down and down. He hated being scolded. He hated being punished. He was afraid to tell his mother what had happened. "What shall I do?" he thought. "I daren't show mother my jacket all torn and muddy like this! I daren't!"

He slipped in at the garden gate and
tiptoed into the house. His mother wasn't
back from seeing Granny. The daily help
was busy getting dinner, and he could hear
her in the kitchen. It was then that the
Very Bad Idea came into his mind.

He tiptoed upstairs. He went to his
cupboard and took down his old jacket.
He took off his muddy new one and put
on the old one. Then he tiptoed downstairs

with the muddy one and went out into the garden. He crumpled up the jacket as small as he could, and flung it over the wall at the bottom of the garden into some thick bushes that grew in the field beyond.

He felt frightened when he had done that, but he felt glad, too. Now nobody would know his new jacket had been spoilt! He wouldn't be scolded. He would get a bicycle for his birthday. He had done a dreadful thing, he knew that, and he knew he was a coward because he had thrown away his jacket instead of

being brave enough to own up that he had spoilt it.

"I don't care!" he kept saying to himself. "I don't care! That sow shouldn't have knocked me over. It's her fault."

It wasn't, of course. He knew perfectly well that he should have put on his old jacket to go and play with Peter. But he was afraid to think that. So he just kept on saying: "I don't care! I don't care!"

Now, the next thing was – how was he to explain the disappearance of his new jacket? He walked into the house, thinking hard. Oh, dear – that would mean making up a story. Alan didn't much like that. He was a truthful boy in the ordinary way. He began to worry about what to say. Oh, what a muddle he was in – one horrid thing always seemed to lead to another!

But things were made unexpectedly easy for him. His mother came in at the front door as he came in at the garden door. "Hallo, Alan!" she called. "So you are just back from Peter's. I'm so glad you put on that old jacket. I forgot to remind you to be sure and wear that to go out to play."

Alan didn't say a word. His mother

came upstairs with him, and stood talking whilst he pulled off his outdoor things. She opened the cupboard door for him to hang up his jacket – and she suddenly saw the new coat wasn't there!

"Good gracious!" she said. "Where's your new jacket? It was there this morning. I saw it. And you've been out all morning at Peter's wearing your *old* one! So somebody must have taken it while you were out. Oh, dear – what can have happened to it?"

She ran to the top of the stairs and called down: "Annie! Has anyone been in the house this morning?"

"No, nobody!" called back Annie. "Well, the window-cleaner came – but he only did the outside of the windows. He didn't come in."

"The window-cleaner!" said Mother. "He must have slipped in at your window, Alan, and opened the cupboard door, seen your new jacket and taken it! I *know* it was there this morning, because I took a dirty hanky out of one of the pockets."

Alan was really scared when he heard all this. His mother saw his frightened

face. "Now, don't you worry about it," she said. "I'll get it back for you. Don't look so scared. The man might have taken more valuable things than that."

"But Mother," began Alan desperately. She didn't hear. She had gone into her own room and was busy looking round to make sure that nothing had been taken from there.

All sorts of things began to happen that weekend. That afternoon a workman walked through the field at the bottom of Alan's garden and caught sight of the crumpled-up mass of cloth in a bush there. He stopped to see what it was.

"Maybe some old coat thrown away by a tramp," he thought, and pulled Alan's jacket out of the bush. He shook it out. It didn't look nice at all, and certainly no one would have thought it was new.

"Dirty and torn – but my missis might clean it up for our young George," thought the workman, and rolled it up under his arm. "I suppose somebody's thrown it away – but what a place to throw it. Littering up the field like that! Still, maybe it will do for young George."

When the mud had dried, George's mother took a brush and brushed the jacket hard. The mud brushed away easily. Then she mended the big tear very neatly

128

indeed, so that it couldn't be seen at all. She called young George to her. He was a bit smaller than Alan, but the jacket looked very nice on him.

"Look at that!" said George's mother to her husband. "I've made a new jacket of it! Plenty of wear in that, you know. What a shame to throw away a jacket as good as that is, just because it was dirty and torn. Well, our George can wear it to school on Monday."

So he did – and it so happened that Alan's mother was going shopping early, just as young George went to school. And she saw the jacket, of course!

She stopped at once and stared as if she couldn't believe her eyes. What! A strange little boy wearing Alan's new jacket. How had he got it?

She went up to George. "Where did you get that jacket?" she asked. George looked astonished.

"My dad found it," he said.

Alan's mother didn't believe that for one moment.

"Is your dad a window-cleaner?" she asked.

"No. He's a bricklayer," said George. "My uncle's the window-cleaner."

"Oho!" thought Alan's mother. "Now I see what happened. The window-cleaner took the jacket, and gave it to his brother. And now here's this boy wearing it – the window-cleaner's nephew!"

She spoke again to George, who by now was feeling scared. "Where do you live and what is your name?"

"I'm George White and I live in Rose Cottage, up on the hill," said George. Then Alan's mother said no more, but walked on quickly.

She went straight to the police station!

She was absolutely certain that George was wearing Alan's jacket which had been stolen by the window-cleaner and passed on to George's father. Well, well, well!

"We'll look into the matter at once, madam," said the policeman at the station. "This man, the window-cleaner, is known as a hard-working and respectable man. It's strange that he should

suddenly steal a jacket."

Alan had gone to school that morning in his old jacket. He had stayed to dinner, and he didn't get home till teatime. He had worried all day long about his spoilt new jacket and wished he hadn't thrown it away. He worried too because his mother had said it might have been stolen by the window-cleaner, and he knew quite well it hadn't.

His mother gave him a terrible shock at teatime. "Well, Alan I've found your jacket!" she said. "I was out shopping, and I suddenly saw young George White wearing it! He's the nephew of that window-cleaner. He told some silly story about his father finding the jacket – finding it indeed! I am sure that it was his uncle who stole it when he came to clean the windows on Saturday, and passed it on to George's family."

Alan went white. He couldn't think of a word to say. His mother went on talking. "So I went to the police station and reported the matter. We shall soon get your jacket back now!"

Alan's father was having tea with them. He suddenly noticed Alan's white frightened face. "What's the matter, Alan?" he said. But before Alan could answer there came a knock at the front door, and Annie came to say that the police sergeant wanted a word with Alan's mother. "Show him in here," said Alan's father, and in came the big sergeant. Alan began to shake at the knees.

"Good evening, madam, good evening, sir," said the sergeant. "About this jacket. Young George's father sticks to it that he found it in the middle of a bush in the field at the bottom of your garden. The window-

cleaner says he knows nothing about the jacket at all."

"But how *could* the jacket have got into the middle of a bush in the field at the bottom of our garden?" began Alan's mother, scornfully. Then her husband stopped her.

"Wait," he said. "It could have got there quite easily. Alan – what do you think about it?"

Alan was shaking. "I f-f-feel sick," he said.

"Well, go on feeling sick," said his father, sternly. "But answer my question. DO YOU HEAR ME?"

There was a dead silence. The police sergeant waited, a notebook in his hand. Alan's mother held her breath. His father looked like a thundercloud.

Alan spoke at last, in a feeble cracking voice that didn't seem a bit like his own. "I threw the jacket there. I got it muddy and torn, and I was afraid of what Mother would say. And I thought you wouldn't give me a bicycle if you knew I'd spoilt my coat."

There was another silence. Then Alan's mother gave a sob. Alan's father turned to the sergeant. "I'm sorry, Sergeant. Tell

young George he can keep the coat. And give this ten-pound note to the window-cleaner, with my sincere apologies for the mistake. I'll deal with Alan myself."

Alan wondered if his father was going to send him to bed early. But he wasn't. He looked sternly and sadly at the frightened boy.

"Don't worry. I'm not going to punish

you. See what an enormous punishment to have brought on yourself! You have lost your new jacket. You have lost your bicycle, because that ten-pound note I gave the sergeant was saved up towards buying it. And you have lost the pride and trust that your mother and I have always had in you. If only you had been brave enough to come and own up that you'd dirtied and torn your jacket, none of this would have happened. You were afraid of a little scolding – and now you have to bear a very big punishment."

Alan's mother put her arms round Alan. "Oh, Alan! I do still trust you! You're not really a coward. You didn't know what awful things happen sometimes when you let yourself be afraid."

"No. I didn't," said poor Alan. "But I know now. It shan't happen again, Mother. Please go on trusting me, please do. I don't mind so much about losing my jacket or my bike – but I do mind dreadfully if you don't trust me any more."

"That's the way to look at it," said his father, looking much less cross. "I'll be proud of you yet!"

Well, I think he's right. Alan was afraid once – but he never will be again.

Amanda
Goes Away

Amanda was Belinda's best doll. She was really very beautiful, for she had curly golden hair, rosy cheeks, a smile that showed very small white teeth and the bluest eyes you ever saw in your life.

She was dressed in blue silk, with little roses sewn round the neck, and round the bottom of the dress. Because she was such a very best doll, Mother only let Belinda have her out when anyone came to tea.

One day Jane and her mummy came to tea. Jane was smaller than Belinda and she was very shy. Belinda got out all her toys to show her, but Jane seemed too shy to look at them.

"Well, I'll show you Amanda then," said Belinda. "Now you just look at Amanda, my Very Best doll, Jane. Don't you think she is beautiful?"

Jane looked at Amanda. Then she looked again. She thought Amanda was the loveliest doll she had ever seen in her life, even lovelier than the doll that sat in the middle of the toy-shop window,

"I like Amanda," said Jane. "Let me hold her."

"Don't drop her, will you?" said Belinda. She gave Amanda to Jane, and the little girl held her tightly. "Oh!" she said, "she's gone to sleep!"

"Her eyes always shut when you make her lie down," said Belinda. "My mummy says she thinks it would be a good idea if real babies always went to sleep like that, too. But they don't. Sit her up, Jane. There, you see she's awake again. Isn't she clever?"

"Yes, she is," said Jane. She wouldn't let Amanda go, even when she had to sit up to tea. She had to sit her down beside her on the chair. Belinda was afraid she would fall, but Jane's mother sat close to Amanda, and she was quite safe.

Now, after tea, the cat came into the nursery. It was a nice cat, and it sat down by the fire to wash itself. Jane didn't see it, and she stepped backwards on to its tail and fell over. The cat put out its claws and scratched Jane's bare arm.

The little girl screamed loudly, and everyone rushed to her. Belinda's mother bathed her arm. Her own mother bound it up. Belinda kept saying how sorry she was.

The cat jumped out of the window. What a to-do there was!

Jane wouldn't stop screaming. She was really very frightened, and her scratch hurt her.

"I'd better take her home," said her mother at last. "Jane, do stop crying, because if you don't people will stare at you in the street and think you have been naughty."

But nothing would make Jane stop screaming and sobbing. And then Belinda had a good idea.

"Look, you're frightening poor Amanda," she said. "Stop crying, Jane, do. You'll make Amanda cry if you don't. Hold her for a minute, won't you?"

Jane stopped crying and looked at Amanda. She thought the doll did look a little bit frightened, and she was sorry. She picked her up and nursed her.

"Well, now you've stopped crying, I think we'll go home!" said Jane's mother. "Come along. We'll get your hat and coat."

Now when Jane was ready she looked at Belinda and said: "I want to take Amanda home with me."

"Oh no," said Belinda, quite shocked at the idea. "You can't. She's my Best doll, my Very Best. She never goes away from me."

"I want her," said Jane, her eyes beginning to fill with tears again. "I'll take care of her and bring her back to-morrow morning."

She began to sob. "Oh dear," said her mother, "do stop, darling. You can't take Amanda. She'd be very unhappy away from Belinda."

"She wouldn't, she wouldn't," sobbed Jane. "She wants to come with me. She said so."

"I didn't hear her," said Belinda, "and I always hear what she says. She sleeps in her little bed at night, Jane. She would

144

miss it dreadfully."

"I've got a little bed she can sleep in," said Jane. "It would just fit her."

"No," said Belinda, and picked up Amanda and held her tightly.

"Listen, darling," said Belinda's mother. "Poor Jane has a bad arm because Pussy scratched her. Let her have Amanda to take home just for tonight. You will have her back tomorrow."

"It might rain, and Amanda would get wet," said Belinda. "She hasn't got a mackintosh or sou'wester. She would get a cold and be ill."

"Darling, it isn't raining," said her mother. "It would do Amanda good to go out and stay."

"Never mind," said Jane's mother. "Don't bother Belinda about it any more. Stop crying, Jane."

Belinda looked at poor Jane, and remembered her arm all done up in bandages. She didn't want to part with Amanda – but Jane did so badly want her.

"All right," said Belinda, pushing Amanda into Jane's arms. "You can have her for one night. But please be kind

to her, and kiss her goodnight and tuck her up."

"Oh yes," said Jane, and she stopped crying at once. "I'll put her in my own doll's bed. Have you got a nightie for her?"

"Yes," said Belinda, and she found it and gave it to Jane. Then Jane said good-bye and thank-you-for-having-me, and she and her mother and Amanda went out of the front door. Belinda climbed up on the windowsill of the nursery and watched them go out of the gate. Jane was carrying Amanda very carefully.

Belinda felt sad. She missed Amanda. Although she hardly ever played with her unless visitors came, Amanda was always in her little bed, looking sweet. Belinda felt sure that the doll was unhappy.

146

When she went to bed, Belinda cried.

"I know Amanda didn't want to go," she sobbed. "I know she didn't. And it's raining now. She'll get wet tomorrow morning and be very ill."

"Don't be silly, darling," said her mother. "She will be having a lovely time, and it may not be raining tomorrow."

But it was. It was simply pouring at breakfast-time. Belinda pointed it out to her mother.

"Amanda will get cold," she said.

"Well, shall I ring and tell Jane to keep her for another day till the rain stops?" said Mother.

"No, thank you," said Belinda. "I want

147

her today." Belinda sat on the nursery windowsill and watched and watched for Jane to come with Amanda. And just as the clock struck ten, Jane came along with her mother. But although she was carrying a doll, it didn't look a bit like Amanda. Amanda was always dressed in blue silk with rosebuds, but this doll seemed to be dressed in red with a red hat. Oh, could anything have happened to Amanda? Or was Jane keeping her and giving Belinda one of her own instead? Belinda simply couldn't bear the thought of that! She flew downstairs.

"You haven't brought back Amanda!" she cried.

"Yes, I have, yes, I have!" said Jane. "Here she is. And look, Mummy has made her a red mackintosh and a red sou'wester out of my old one, because it was raining. Doesn't she look really sweet? She was as good as gold last night, Belinda. She slept all night long and she was so happy. She told me she was."

Belinda looked at Amanda. Amanda looked back at her with her usual sweet smile. She looked really lovely in the red mackintosh and red sou'wester. Jane's mummy had made them beautifully.

"Oh!" said Belinda, joyfully, "it's just what she wanted. I never could take her out in the rain because she hadn't even a coat. Now I can take her out this very morning. Can't I, Mother?"

"Of course," said Mother. "And you

can put on your own red mackintosh and sou'wester, too, which almost match Amanda's. Everyone will know you are mother and daughter – that *will* be nice for you!" So out went Belinda in her red mac and sou'wester.

"I *am* glad I lent you to Jane for the night, after all!" she told Amanda. "I didn't want to, but I did, and now we've both got a lovely reward. Aren't we lucky, Amanda?"

And Belinda was quite certain that Amanda nodded her head!

Simple Simon
Goes Shopping

"Now, Simple Simon," said his mother. "You try and be a sensible boy today and help me. I am really busy."

"Yes, Mother," said Simple Simon. "I won't do a single thing wrong."

"Put the kettle on the gas-stove to boil," said Mother. "That's the first thing you can do."

So Simon did. After a while his mother called to him. "Is that kettle boiling yet, Simon?"

Simon went to see.

"No, Mother," he shouted. "It's not."

"Is there steam coming out of the spout?" called his mother.

"No," said Simon. "There isn't."

"Funny!" said his mother. "It's ages since you put it on to boil."

She came out to see if it had begun to

boil – and she looked first at the kettle then at Simon.

"Did you expect the kettle to boil if you didn't light the gas?" she said. "Simon, either you don't use your brains, or you haven't got any. I can't make up my mind which."

"I'm sorry, Mother," said Simon, and lighted the gas. But his mother was still cross with him. Simon didn't like that. He went to her.

"Mother, tell me to do something else

for you," he said. "I'll do that really well, I truly will."

"There's nothing you don't make a muddle over," said his mother, crossly.

"I could go and do some shopping for you," said Simon.

"You went shopping on Wednesday, and what did you do?" said his mother. "You took your shoes to the fish-shop to be mended!"

"Well, there was a notice up that said 'Soles for Sale'," said Simon. "How was I to know that the soles they meant were fish? You told me to get new soles put on my shoes."

"And yesterday I sent you for some soap and you brought home a tin of soup," said his mother.

"Well, I thought you said soup," said Simon. "Mother, do let me go shopping again. I promise I'll be very sensible."

"All right," said his mother. "Go to the grocer's, and bring back the groceries. There will be a box of matches, a box of custard powder, a bottle of vinegar, and a packet of butter. Now don't break the bottle of vinegar, and

don't spill the custard powder."

"Mother, I won't," said Simon, earnestly. "You shall see what a very good sensible boy I can be."

"The custard powder is important," said Mother. "I want it for our dinner. Go along now, and take the basket."

Simon trotted off happily. It was nice to be trusted. Very nice. He would be so sensible. He would bring back everything, and nothing would be spilt or sat on.

He went to the grocer's and got all the goods. He put them into his basket. Yes – the box of matches, the box of

custard powder, the bottle of vinegar, the butter. Good!

"I'll go home through the fields," he said to himself. "It will be nice to walk by the stream. The buttercups are out, too – they will look so pretty." So Simon started off home, and climbed over the stile to get through the buttercup field. He walked through the buttercups, and came to the stream. Then he happened to look down his legs, and he was very upset.

"My shoes and my socks are covered with yellow powder!" he said. "I must have spilt the custard powder – and Mother

asked me not to. Oh dear, oh dear! What a nuisance."

He set down his basket and brushed off the yellow powder. He didn't know it was pollen from the buttercups! He stood and wondered what to do. Should he tell his mother he had spilt some? She would be very cross. But she would be crosser still if he didn't tell her, and she found the box half empty.

"I'd better tell her," said poor Simon,

with a sigh. "Oh dear – I suppose the lid came off the box."

He set off home again, going through the buttercups once more, and, of course, the buttercup pollen spilt all over his shoes and socks again!

Simon didn't know he had left his basket behind him by the stream. He was so anxious to get home and tell his mother, that he forgot to pick it up and bring it. Oh dear!

He got home and ran to find his mother. He saw that his legs were all yellow again, and he began to cry. "Mother! Don't be cross. I've spilt the custard powder all over my legs! Look!" His mother looked. It did seem like custard powder. She was cross.

"How did that happen? Where's the basket? The lid must have come off the custard powder, and the powder must have trickled out through the cracks of the basket. Careless boy! Where's the basket, Simon?"

"Oh – I've left it by the stream!" said Simon, suddenly remembering. "Oh, mother, I've left it behind. But how could I have spilt custard powder over my legs,

then, if I didn't have the basket? I brushed my shoes and socks clean, I know I did."

"Go and get the basket," said his mother, crossly. "Someone else will find it. Hurry, Simon!"

Simon hurried, puzzling about how the custard powder could have got on his legs again, when he *wasn't* carrying the basket. He came to the stream – and oh, what a good thing, there was the basket!

He went to pick it up. He thought he would see if the lid of the custard *had* come off, so he tipped everything out. The box of matches rolled down the bank to the water, and fell in, plop!

"Bother!" said Simon, and fished out the box. It was dripping wet. He put it back

into the basket. He sat down to brush off the powder from his legs – and, oh dear, what was that underneath him? The butter, of course!

"Why did you have to be just underneath me?" said Simon angrily to the butter. A wasp smelt the butter and flew down to see what it was. Simon slapped at it.

The wasp stung him. Simon howled loudly, but there was no one to comfort him. He looked at his hand where the wasp had stung him. He remembered that his mother put vinegar on wasp-stings, so he opened the bottle, and poured it all over his hand.

"There!" he said. "What a good thing I had some vinegar with me. Now my hand won't swell up."

He put the squashed butter, the empty bottle of vinegar and the custard powder back into the basket with the wet match-box. Then he set off home once more and was dismayed to see his legs covered with yellow powder again.

"I should think every bit of the custard is spilt now," he thought. "What will Mother say?"

He called for her, feeling very sorry for himself. "Mother, where are you? I found the basket, and here it is."

"Oh, good boy!" said his mother,

pleased, and came to get it. She took out the matches.

"Gracious, Simon, they're wet – no use at all! They'll never strike now! What in the world have you done to them?"

"Well, you see, they fell into the river," said Simon.

His mother took out the butter and looked at it.

"I suppose you sat on it, after I'd *begged* you not to!" she said.

"Well, Mother it happened to be underneath me when I sat down," said Simon. "I didn't *mean* to sit on it. It just let itself be sat on."

"I see," said his mother. "And look here – what about this bottle of vinegar? It's empty!"

"Oh, yes, Mother; you see a wasp stung me and I poured the vinegar over my hand," said Simon. "I thought that was clever of me, to remember to put vinegar on a sting."

"Well it wasn't very clever to put the whole bottle on," said Mother crossly. "And now here's the custard powder. I suppose the box will be empty!"

Simon stared dolefully at the box. But to his surprise, when his mother opened it, it was chock-full!

"Well, look there!" said Mother. "After

all the fuss you made about having custard powder all over your shoes and socks, and rushing home without the basket to tell me, you didn't spill any after all!"

"But Mother – I did! Look at my legs!" said Simon. "Isn't that custard powder?"

His mother looked very carefully. Then she laughed.

"It's *buttercup* powder," she said. "You walked through the buttercups, didn't you? Well, they always spill their yellow pollen on you if you brush against them. You didn't spill the custard powder at all."

"Well, I'm a very good boy then, after all!" said Simon, pleased.

"Oh, no, you're not!" said his mother. "Who wetted the matches? Who sat on the butter? Who used up all my vinegar? A silly, naughty boy did that! You tell me his name!"

But Simon didn't want to. He went out by himself and told the buttercups what he thought of them.

"Spilling your custard powder all down my legs!" he said to them. "You ought to be ashamed of yourselves!"

They nodded their golden heads at him.

They didn't care! Poor old Simple Simon, he never can get things right.

The
Old Bicycle

Peter had a long way to go to school each morning. It took him half an hour to get there, so he had to start very early.

Some of the children went to school on bicycles, and Peter wished he could too. So when his birthday came near he asked his mother if she thought she could get him one.

"Mother, couldn't I possibly have one?" he begged. "It would save me so much time. I get quite tired walking such a long way."

"Peter, you can't ride a bicycle, so it's silly to ask for one," said his mother.

This was quite true. Peter couldn't ride. He could ride Marjorie's tricycle, and he could easily pedal along in Jim's little motor-car – but he couldn't ride a bicycle.

So he made up his mind to learn. On

Saturday morning he went round to Jimmy's house and asked him if he could try to ride his bicycle.

"How do you ride it without falling off?" he asked.

"Well, if I were you, I'd try putting your right foot on the left pedal first, and use the bicycle like a scooter," said Jimmy. "Take hold of the handles – that's right – now put your foot on the left pedal – yes, like that. Now, off you go. Push yourself along with your left foot, and try to get your balance."

So off went Peter round the garden, and he soon found that he could keep his balance very well like that. Then he put

his right foot across to the right pedal, and the left foot on the left pedal and tried to see if he could balance like that too, with no foot on the ground at all. He couldn't at first and over he went. But he didn't hurt himself.

He tried again and again. He had to go home when dinnertime came. Jimmy said he could come in the afternoon and try again.

Well, it really wasn't very long before Peter had taught himself to ride on Jimmy's bike, and he was very pleased about it.

"Now Mother can't say I don't know how to ride!" he thought. So he spoke to her again.

167

"Mother, I can ride a bicycle now. I've learnt on Jimmy's. I can ride beautifully. So may I have a bicycle for my birthday, please?"

"Well, I'll talk to Daddy," said Mother. "But bicycles are very expensive things to buy, you know, Peter, and we haven't very much money."

Mother spoke to Daddy that night, and the next day she told Peter what his father had said.

"Daddy says he can't possibly afford to buy you a bicycle," she said. "I'm sorry, Peter dear, because I know you'll be dreadfully disappointed after learning to ride – but it's no use expecting Daddy to buy you one, so don't hope for it."

Peter *was* disappointed. He didn't say a word but he went up to his bedroom and screwed up his eyes to stop any tears from coming out. After all, he was soon going to be nine and he was far too big to cry about anything.

When his birthday came his mother gave him a fine box of soldiers and his father gave him a book about aeroplanes. "Sorry about the bicycle, old son," said

Daddy. "I'd give it to you if I could, you know that. But I just can't afford it. I'm afraid you must go on walking to school."

Now that very morning something happened to Peter. He was walking to school as usual when he saw a boy coming along on a bicycle. The bicycle was small and the boy was big. Just as the boy got near to Peter, a dog ran across the road in front of the bicycle.

The boy swerved but the dog ran right into him. Over went the boy with a crash on to the ground, and the bicycle fell on

top of him, its wheels spinning in the air!
The dog gave a yelp and fled for its life.

Peter ran to help the boy up. But the
boy could not stand.

"I've hurt my leg," he said. "I do hope
it's not broken. Can you drag me to the
side of the road?"

So Peter dragged him to the side and the boy took down his sock and looked at his poor leg. "It hurts dreadfully," he said. Peter knew that it must, because the big boy had tears in his eyes. No big boys ever cried unless they really couldn't help it.

"What shall I do?" said Peter. "Where do you live?"

"Well, my father is Dr Johns," said the boy. "I'm Adam Johns. If you could possibly go to my home and catch my father before he starts out on his rounds, he could come along here at once in the car. But you'll have to be quick, because he is starting out early this morning."

"But your house is ever so far!" said Peter. "It will take me ages to get there, even if I run."

"Can you ride a bike?" asked Adam. "If you can, see if mine is all right. It doesn't look as if I smashed anything when I fell over."

"Yes, I can ride," said Peter. "I've never ridden in the road before, but I can be careful. I'll go right away now and see if I can catch your father. Goodbye!"

Peter jumped on to Adam's bicycle.

"Just be careful now!" shouted Adam. "I don't want *you* to have an accident too!"

Peter was careful. He rode well to the left of the road, and didn't take any risks at all. The bicycle was just the right size for him. It seemed rather an old one, for the paint was worn off, and the bright parts were rusty. Part of the rubber of the left pedal was missing, and the right brake wouldn't work. But it was lovely to ride a bicycle, even though it was an old one. Peter rang his bell at the corners, and at last came to Dr Johns' house. The doctor was just stepping into his car to go to see a patient.

Peter rode up, ringing his bell as loudly

as possible. The doctor turned round.

"Wait a minute, wait a minute!" shouted Peter. "I've a message for you."

Then he jumped off the bicycle and told the doctor what had happened to Adam. The doctor listened with a grave face. "What a good thing you were able to ride a bicycle!" he said. "You'd better ride to school on it this morning or you will be late. Thank you for your help.

I'll go straight to Adam now."

He set off in his car. Peter rode to school being very careful indeed not to go too fast because of the broken brake.

He rode home on the bicycle too, and Mother was most astonished to see him arriving at the gate on a bicycle.

"Where did you get that from?" she asked. Peter told her.

"Mother, could I have my dinner quickly so that I can ride the bike back to Dr Johns and ask how Adam is?" he said. "Then I can leave the bicycle there and walk to school in good time."

"Very well," said his mother. "But don't gobble or you'll be ill!"

Peter soon finished his dinner. Then he went to his bookshelf and looked along his books. He thought perhaps Adam might like a book to read if he had to rest his leg – and perhaps he would like a jigsaw puzzle to do, too.

He put a book in the bicycle basket and a jigsaw puzzle. Then off he went, ringing the bell merrily at the corners. He soon came to Adam's house. He put the bicycle in the front garden and rang the door bell.

The daily help showed him into the drawing-room, and in a moment Adam's mother came into the room.

"You must be the boy who so kindly helped Adam this morning!" she said. "Thank you very much indeed."

"How is Adam's leg?" asked Peter.

"I'm afraid it is broken," said Mrs Johns. "But not very badly. And as you fetched help so quickly, it was set almost at once and will soon be mended."

"I've brought Adam a book to read, and a puzzle," said Peter. "I'm really awfully

sorry his leg is broken."

"Oh, how kind you are!" said Mrs Johns. "Come and see Adam. He is in his playroom."

Peter was taken to see Adam. The big boy had a fine playroom with an electric railway running all round it.

It looked most exciting. Peter had a clockwork railway, but the electric one looked wonderful.

"Hallo!" said Adam. "Did you hear my leg was broken? No wonder it hurt me!"

Peter gave Adam what he had brought. The two boys talked hard. "You must come after tea and set my electric train going," said Adam.

"Well, I would," said Peter, "but I'd have to walk, you see, and I'd never have time to get here and back and do my homework too. I haven't got a bike like you."

"Haven't you?" said Mrs Johns. "Well – Adam is having a new, much bigger bicycle for his birthday next week, and we were wondering what to do with his old one. Perhaps you would like to have it?"

"Good idea!" said Adam. "Then you can

come and see me every day! Yes – you have it, Peter. I can't ride for some weeks, and by that time my new bike will have arrived. So I can give you my old one with pleasure. You were jolly kind to me and you deserve it!"

Peter was red with delight. "I shall have to ask my mother first," he said. "But I'm sure she'll say yes. Oh, I say – I have so badly wanted a bike, and now I've got one! I'll ride home on it and see what Mother says!"

Mother said yes, of course! "You've been a good boy and not grumbled because we couldn't give you a bicycle for your birthday," she said, "and now that your own kindness has brought you one, I am certainly not going to say no. You may have it, and Daddy and I will get the brake mended for you, and a new rubber for the pedal, and have it all re-painted. Then it will be as good as new!"

Well, you should see that old bicycle now! It looks just like a new one, and Peter keeps it so bright and shining. He is very proud of it and rides on it to school every day.

"Your accident brought me two things!" he said to Adam. "It brought me a bicycle – and a friend. Shan't we have fun together when your leg is better, Adam!"

The
Loose Shoe Button

"Alice! Is your shoe-button coming off?"
Mother said, looking down at Alice's
right shoe.

Alice looked too, though she knew quite
well that the button *was* loose. "Oh yes,
it's just about to come off," said Alice,
who guessed what Mother was going to
say next.

"Now, Alice, do remember to sew
it on before you go to school tomorrow
morning," said Mother. "You are so bad at
remembering little things like that."

"Oh, Mother, won't you sew it on for
me?" begged Alice.

"Really, Alice! Don't you remember
what you promised me when I gave you
your beautiful new work-basket?" said
Mother. "You promised me faithfully that
you would keep your clothes mended –

darn your socks, sew on your buttons, and keep yourself really tidy! You can easily sew on that button."

"All right," said Alice sulkily. "But, Mother, I've a dreadful lot of work to do tonight, because I am going in for an important exam tomorrow, you know – and I've got to look up all those history dates and French words."

"It will take you at the very most two minutes to sew on that button," said Mother, getting cross. "Why do you put things off so, Alice? You are supposed to

181

be a clever girl at school – and yet I have to grumble at you nearly every day for leaving some silly little thing undone. Now do be a good girl and put that button on AT ONCE."

"Very well, Mother," said Alice, and she went to fetch her work-basket. But on the way she met the black kitten, who was really the most playful thing in the world. So of course Alice stopped to play with it, and when she had finished, she had forgotten all about her work-basket!

She sat down to do her work. She was a

clever girl, and had such a good memory that she only had to look at a thing once to know it. She was very, very lucky. No lesson was any trouble to her and Alice felt quite certain that she would be top in the exam and beat all the other girls by about a hundred marks!

She swung her foot under the table as she learnt her history dates: "1066, 1087," she said to herself. "How easy all this is! I can't imagine why that silly little Mary Yates always gets her dates wrong."

As she swung her foot she felt that her shoe was loose. She remembered the button.

"Bother!" she said. "I forgot to sew on

that button! Well, I'd better go and do it now. Oh no, I won't – it's too much bother. I'll do it in the morning."

So Alice didn't sew on the button, and she went to bed with the button hanging by a thread on her shoe under the chair. She fell asleep at once and dreamt that she worked out all her exam papers most perfectly, and that she had top marks and a most wonderful prize. The prize was an enormous doll, and Alice was just holding

out her arms to take it when she heard a voice speaking to her.

"Alice! It's time to get up! Hurry, because it is your exam morning and you mustn't miss the bus to school."

Alice stretched herself and yawned. It was warm and cosy in bed. She didn't want to get up a bit. So she lay there and snoozed until Mother came along and pulled all the clothes off her. Then she *had* to get up.

When she put on her shoes, she remembered the loose button again. It really was almost off now! Bother!

"I meant to get up a bit early and sew it on," thought Alice crossly. "Now I shan't have time unless I gobble my breakfast – and that will make Mother cross."

She did eat her breakfast quite quickly, though, and when she looked at the clock she thought she would just have time to sew on the button. But then Mother said that she really must go upstairs and put clean hair-ribbons on because hers were so crumpled and dirty.

"Oh dear! Now I shan't have time to sew on that silly button!" thought Alice as she ran upstairs. "No – it's no good. I shall miss the bus if I wait to do it."

She set off to catch the bus at the corner of the road, swinging her school-bag as she went. Then she suddenly saw the bus coming and she began to run. It would never, never do to miss it on exam morning!

As she ran, the button on her shoe came right off! It rolled into the gutter and was lost. Of course the shoe wouldn't stay on Alice's foot without the button to hold the

strap – so the shoe came off too! Alice was running fast and she didn't feel that her shoe had come off until she had left it a little way behind.

"Oh dear!" cried Alice, stopping. "The bus will go without me – but I *must* get my shoe! I can't go to school with only one shoe. Oh, bus, stop, stop! Wait for me!"

She rushed back to get her shoe and she put it on again. Then she began to run once more – but it is quite impossible to run fast with a buttonless shoe, and Alice had to half run, half shuffle, in case she

lost her shoe again.

And the bus didn't wait for her! It was already one minute late and it couldn't stop for Alice. So off it went up the road, round the corner, and out of sight.

Alice sat down on the bus-seat and cried. She cried bitterly, because she knew there was no bus now for two hours and she couldn't get to school in time to sit for her exam.

"If only I could sit for the exam, I'd be top, I know," she sobbed. "And I could go to the big school in the next town, and because I had passed the Entrance Exam Mother and Daddy wouldn't have to pay any school fees for me, and I could have nicer dresses and perhaps a bicycle. Now I shan't be able to sit for the exam at all!"

Alice was so upset that at first she couldn't even get up to walk home. But at last she did, and Mother *was* astonished to see a tear-stained face looking round the door.

"Alice! Whatever has happened?" she cried.

Alice sobbed everything out. "I didn't sew on that button – and my shoe came

off and I missed the bus – and there isn't another one and I shall be late for the exam, and I shan't pass the Entrance Exam."

Mother was wise. She didn't scold Alice. She saw that the little girl had been too well punished by her buttonless shoe to need any more scolding. She just looked sad and solemn and took Alice on to her knee.

"Sometimes, Alice, to be forgetful in a little thing will spoil a much bigger thing," she said. "I am very sorry for you. I will ring for a taxi to take you to school. Then maybe you will be in time for the exam."

"Oh, Mother! I don't deserve it, but I do, do wish you would," said Alice, cheering up. So Mother rang up to see if the taxi-cab could come. But it was already out, taking someone to the station. The garage man said that as soon as the cab came back again it should fetch Alice.

The little girl had to wait half an hour before the taxi came. She had time to think of all the things she had put off doing, all the things she had forgotten – just little tiny things that didn't seem really to matter very much. And they did matter after all.

Alice was an hour and a half late for

school. The children were in the middle of their second exam. Alice took her papers and sat down. She worked very, very hard indeed.

But alas for poor Alice! She had missed the history exam altogether, so she had no marks for that at all – and little Mary Yates came out top of everyone, and passed the exam for herself. Alice was dreadfully disappointed, and she cried in bed that night till she soaked her pillow and Mother had to get a clean pillow-case.

"Now listen, Alice," said Mother, putting the clean pillow-case on the pillow. "You have still another year at this school, and one more chance of taking the exam. You have good brains and can easily pass it. See that the little things don't spoil the big things again. It is no use having brains if you don't use them to sew on a loose button as well as to learn all the history dates there are!"

"Mother, I promise I'll never forget things again," said Alice. And she meant it. Next year she will probably pass that exam – but who would have thought that a loose shoe-button would have caused such a terrible disappointment!

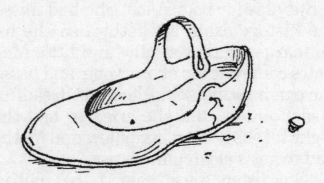